Disney · PIXAR

Cars

MATER IN PARIS

By Frank Berrios
Based on a story by Henry Jakob

Illustrated by Scott Tilley, Andrew Phillipson, Janelle Bell-Martin,
Seung Beom Kim, and the Disney Storybook Artists

Random House 🏠 New York

ISBN: 978-0-7364-2875-0
randomhouse.com/kids
MANUFACTURED IN CHINA
10 9 8 7 6 5 4 3 2

Mater and Lizzie were listening to the radio one afternoon. Suddenly, the music stopped and Mater heard the voice of Holley Shiftwell, the British secret agent!

"Hello, Mater! Can you hear me?" asked Holley over the radio.

"Holley, is that you?" asked Mater.

"Yes," Holley replied. "Finn and I are in Paris tracking some Lemons, and no one knows more about Lemons than you do. Will you come join the mission?"

"Sure thing," said Mater. "But how will I get to Paris?"

"Siddeley is already on his way to get you," Holley said.

Mater looked up as Siddeley came in for a landing right on Main Street.
"I'm going on a top-secret mission to Paris," Mater whispered to Lightning.
"You wanna come, too?"
"Paris? Um, sure," said Lightning, staring at the plane.
"*Hooo-wee!* Me and Lightning are a super-secret spy team!" yelled Mater.

In Paris, Mater and Lightning discussed the mission with Finn and Holley.

"The Lemons keep giving us the slip," said Holley. "What would you do if you were a Lemon, Mater?"

"Well, I'd be looking to get me some spare parts," replied Mater.

"Brilliant!" said Finn. "You and Lightning can visit Tomber, the spare-parts dealer. Holley and I will check the market across town for more clues."

When Mater and Lightning reached Tomber's garage, the three-wheeled car was upset.

"I've been robbed!" he exclaimed. "Two crates of valuable spare parts are missing!"

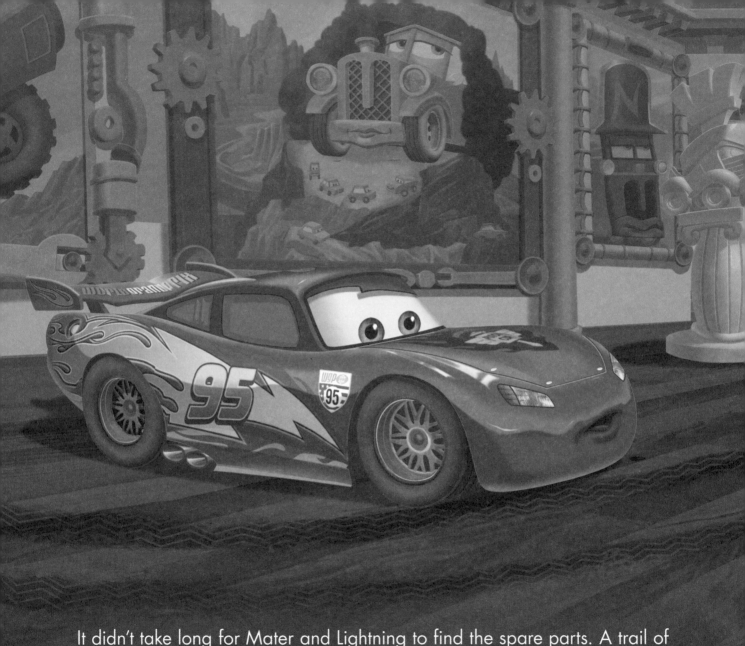

It didn't take long for Mater and Lightning to find the spare parts. A trail of them led from Tomber's garage to the Louvre, the most famous museum in Paris. As Mater and Lightning cruised through the museum, they spotted a puddle. "Eww, somebody's leaking oil," said Lightning.

"This oil is old and grimy," Mater said. "It could've come from a Lemon. And these tire tracks sure look a lot like the treads on a Hugo!"

"Then I guess we know what kind of Lemons we're looking for," Lightning said. "Hugos!"

Mater and Lightning followed the oily tire tracks to a nearby café.
"Them cars right there is Hugos!" gasped Mater, recognizing the
Lemons even though they were in disguise.
"Try to act casual," whispered Lightning.

Lightning and Mater followed the Hugos to the famous Moteur Rouge nightclub, but the Lemons realized they were being trailed.

"We gotta lose those two," said one of the Hugos, glancing back at Mater and Lightning.

The Hugos darted through the club and made their way backstage.
"C'mon, buddy, we can't let them get away!" yelled Mater.
But both Lightning and Mater slammed on their brakes when the
Hugos drove onto the stage with the car-car dancers!

"What do we do now?" asked Lightning.

"We gotta blend in!" replied Mater. Mater and Lightning put on feathered headdresses, kicked up their tires, and danced across the stage. The crowd loved them!

Mater and Lightning chased the Hugos to the top of the Eiffel Tower, where they tipped over and passed out!

"I knew those Hugos couldn't outrun us," said Mater. "We wore 'em down!"

"All in a day's work for Super Spy Mater!" replied Lightning, smiling.

When Holley and Finn arrived, they were amazed to see two beat-up Hugos sporting shiny new exhaust pipes and tubing!

"You recovered all of Tomber's stolen spare parts!" said Holley.

"Awww, it was nothin'," replied Mater shyly.

After the Paris police towed the Hugos away, Lightning, Mater, Finn, and Holley went for a cruise around the city.

"Anybody up for a little snack?" asked Mater.

"Paris has some of the finest fuels in the world," replied Holley.

"That's what I'm talkin' 'bout!" said Mater, revving his engine. "Last one there pays the bill!"

As they crossed the finish line, each racer thought he had won. But the judges declared a tie!

"I guess we'll have to race again," said Lightning. "But this time, we'll do it in Radiator Springs!"

"Agreed!" replied Francesco. "Francesco will enjoy beating Lightning in his hometown."

"I'd sure like to see you try," said Lightning, and he and Francesco sped toward the airport.

The second leg of the race was held at the Monza Racetrack.
When the two cars entered the track, Lightning took the lead.
"Stay focused," Lightning said to himself, looking straight
ahead and putting the pedal to the metal.

Finally, the day of the big race arrived.
"And they're off!" yelled the announcer at the start of the race.
Francesco took the first turn at full speed, but surprisingly, he didn't spin out of control. Lightning laughed when he noticed that Francesco was wearing new treaded tires. Maybe he had taught Francesco too well!

The racers stopped for a rest beneath an olive tree.
Francesco sighed. "Ah, Italy is beautiful, no? Just like Francesco!"
Lightning chuckled. "Do you always think about yourself?" he asked.
"Of course," said Francesco. "On the racetrack, Francesco thinks only about himself and doing his best. This is why he always wins!"

Francesco poured on the speed and caught up to Lightning but nearly spun off the road!

"How do you make these left turns so well?" asked Francesco.

"An old friend taught me that practice makes perfect," said Lightning. "But treaded tires help, too."

Before Francesco could finish, Lightning took off down the road.
"Ka-*ciao*, Francesco!" yelled Lightning.
"Ha! Lightning pulled a fast one on you," Mater said.

"How about a little warm-up before the big race?" asked Lightning after lunch.
"A warm-up?" said Francesco. "Francesco is already warm, but he understands
that Lightning needs some practice. Francesco would be happy to—"

"Hmph! Francesco has many more fans than Lightning McQueen!" exclaimed Francesco as he spun his wheels to autograph two stacks of photos at the same time!

As Lightning made his way out of the airport, he slowed down to meet his eager fans. Mater got the cars to line up, and Luigi made sure they all got a photo with their racing hero. Lightning's fans chanted: "Light-ning! Light-ning!"

After Lightning McQueen and Francesco Bernoulli each won a race in the World Grand Prix, they decided to hold a tiebreaker race in Francesco's hometown in Italy.

"Welcome to Monza—the best city in the world!" said Francesco.

REMATCH!

By Frank Berrios
Based on a story by Susan Amerikaner

Illustrated by Scott Tilley, Andrew Phillipson, Janelle Bell-Martin,
Dan Gracey, Seung Beom Kim, and the Disney Storybook Artists

Random House 🏠 New York

Materials and characters from the movie *Cars 2*. Copyright © 2013 Disney/Pixar.
Disney/Pixar elements © Disney/Pixar, not including underlying vehicles owned by third parties;
and, if applicable: FIAT is a trademark of FIAT S.p.A. All rights reserved. Published in the United States by
Random House Children's Books, a division of Random House, Inc., 1745 Broadway, New York, NY 10019,
and in Canada by Random House of Canada Limited, Toronto, in conjunction with Disney Enterprises, Inc.

ISBN: 978-0-7364-2875-0
randomhouse.com/kids
MANUFACTURED IN CHINA
10 9 8 7 6 5 4 3 2